THE OLYMPI

BOOK I

SON

OF

SPARTAPUSS

ROBIN PRICE

THE OLYMPUSS GAMES

BOOK I: SON OF SPARTAPUSS

First published by Mogzilla in 2014

Paperback edition:
ISBN: 9781906132811

www.mogzilla.co.uk

Printed in Malta

Author's dedication:
'For Scarlet and Indigo.'

Illustrator's dedication:
'For Lorna, Brendan and Barney.'

THE SECRET DIARY OF THE SON OF SPARTAPUSS

MAUIS IV

May 4th

Roman holiday? Not for me! It's my first night in the biggest city in the whole Feline Empire. But mother says I've got to stay in and clean the villa. She works me harder than a chariot dog. Listen... that's her calling again. What does she want now?

MAUIS V

May 5th

More jobs today. "Tidy your basket!" "Clean your claws, miaow miaow miaow miaow miaow!"

I thought mother was never going to let me out to see the sights. When I finally escaped, the first thing on my list was the most famous street in Rome – The Appian Way. It turns out that it's just a dusty road with a market at the end of it. I came across a young female sitting by a wooden cage.

Her orange eyes burned like temple lamps.

"Stop staring at me!" she hissed.

"I can stare at you if I like," I replied. "I'm a free cat."

"How nice for you!" she snapped.

Then I noticed the iron chain attached to her foot. "I'm a stray. I'm not allowed to talk to you unless you've come to buy."

"Buy?" I asked. "What's for sale?"

Her orange eyes flashed again.

"I am for sale!" she hissed. "You Romans captured me and dragged me here. But that wasn't enough. Now you want to stare at me as well."

She muttered something under her breath in the language of the Squeaks. Father made me take Squeak lessons, so I understood what she said. I can't write down what she called me, it's too rude.

"There's no need for bad language," I said – then I wished I hadn't. It sounded like the sort of thing my father would say.

"You Romans are all so *terribly* polite," she purred in a mocking voice, "invading other countries. Stealing their treasure. Capturing free cats and selling them as 'strays'. Making them work as your slaves. You act as if Rome owns the whole world!"

"Er, it kind of does actually," I replied.

She didn't answer. She just stared at me. That was a sure sign that she liked me.

"I'm late. I've got things to do," I said. Then I picked up my bag and went off.

On the way home some locals padded over and started hissing at me. Perhaps it was because I'm ginger? Or maybe it was because I'm a foreigner from the Land of the Kitons? I went for the biggest one first. He tried to scratch my nose but I dodged the blow and got my claws out. Then I went for him. I won't go into details but five seconds later he was rolling around on the floor begging for his mother. Sorry diary – lying to you is like lying to myself. Actually, those locals gave me a beating. What could I do? There were three of them! At least I didn't run away.

Mother made a terrible fuss when she saw my ears were torn up, again. She hates it when I get into fights.

She told me that she has hired a new 'tutor' – a teacher who is going to give me lessons in my home. I told her that my real 'home' is far away in the Land of the Kitons. I'm twelve summers old now. What more is there to learn?

MAUIS VI
May 6th

Mother keeps ordering me around. "Clean your bowl, keep your tail clean, lick behind your ears, miaow miaow miaow miaow miaow miaow miaow!" She's fiercer than Fleanus on a bad fur day. She treats me as if my eyes were still closed, like a helpless little kitten!

"Go to the market and get some fish for supper," she ordered. "I'm trusting you, so don't get into any more trouble."

"Yes mother," I replied.

"And make sure you're back soon."

I would normally have made an excuse but I decided to go to the market for mother.

I am saving up for a lyre. I can't actually play the lyre. Mother thinks it's too difficult. But I'm a fast learner. Plus, if I carry an instrument around, everyone will know how interesting I am. I wonder if that fiery female will still be at the market?

MAUIS VII
May 7th

Lots more to write about today. I went back to the place in the market where they sell the strays. It took ages to retrace my steps. They sell everything from fried squid to scratching posts. I finally found my orange-eyed female by the mouse kebab stall. She was still wearing that chain on her leg. This time she was also wearing an iron collar. When I padded up to her, she looked at me in a strange way.

"You again Roman?" she purred softly. "Are you rich?"

For some reason, I didn't tell her that I'm not actually a Roman, I'm from the Land of the Kitons. I'm not sure why I held this back – perhaps I like pretending to be somebody else. Sometimes it doesn't feel so good to come from a dark island in the far north of the Feline Empire.

"Answer me, I won't bite!" she said.

"My family are rich," I replied.

This isn't exactly true but we probably ARE rich compared to her family. She grew up in a mud hut, most likely.

"Roman," she began, "can I ask you something?"

"What?" I replied.

"Nothing," she said. "Forget it."

She fixed me with those big eyes again. They were as full as the hunter's moon.

"I was wondering if you might like to buy me," she whispered.

I didn't know what to say. Finally, I opened my mouth.

"What?!" I gasped.

Then I realised that I sounded a bit rude. "I mean... how much. How much are they selling you for?" I asked.

"I don't know how much. It's an auction," she explained.

I nodded, but she knew I didn't understand.

"An auction – where the buyers keep naming a higher price until the one with the most money wins. This market is famous for its auctions."

"I don't come here much," I replied.

"I bet your slaves probably do all of your shopping for you, don't they? All of you Romans are as rich as kings," she laughed.

"What time are they selling you?"

"Tomorrow at noon," she replied.

"I'd better go," I said. "My mother will be climbing the walls."

Then I wished I hadn't said that. I say some fluff-witted things sometimes. I could bite myself!

"If you have to go, then go," she said sadly. "I'll look out for you in the crowd tomorrow at the auction."

"You'd better be there!" she hissed.

MAUIS IX

May 9th

Well diary, it's not every day that you make a new friend and she asks you to buy her! If my father found out, he'd go spitting mad. He's got some strange ideas about strays. He doesn't approve of them. But she looked so sad in that iron chain. My new lyre will have to wait. Luckily I've been saving up. I have four silver denarii – which is a lot of money.

I only had one thing on my mind – the sale. I had to be at the market by noon. I grabbed my money bag from its hiding place under my basket and I padded slowly out of my room. As I stalked across the courtyard, I heard a familiar voice calling me.

"Get down here! Your tutor is waiting!" hissed my mother.

Then I heard another voice. It sounded high pitched. Maybe it was my tutor?

I shot through the archway like a stone from a sling. I could feel my mother's eyes burning into my back as I ran. Soon I was lost in a spider-web of winding streets.

The market started at noon, so I had to hurry. I was held up behind long lines of red-crested soldiers. Their shields and helmets gleamed in the blazing sun. Roman soldiers don't usually look this smart. They were on their way to cheer the Emperor Nero as he paraded around on Paws Field. Over here, they call it a 'triumph'.

I wanted to push ahead through the lines but you don't want to mess with the Roman army – they call themselves 'the Sons of Paws'. Paws is the Roman God of War so I was careful not to annoy them.

I padded on with the sun on my back and a thick layer of dust on my coat. Finally I arrived at a place where some fish sellers were shouting out their prices. Wooden cart wheels clattered against the stones.

I fought my way through the crowd, past the dormouse kebab sellers. Their food smelled delicious. Finally, I came to the spot where my new friend's cage stood.

"I've made it!" I announced breathlessly, popping my head through the wooden bars. But to my horror, the cage was empty. In a panic I sniffed the air and looked around.

"The stray!" I moaned in despair. "She's gone! Where have they taken her?"

'Where do you think? You ginger half-wit!" replied an ancient tabby with yellow teeth. He was pointing towards a row of wooden posts where a small crowd had gathered.

All of the strays for sale that day were lined up in a row for the customers to inspect.

As I approached the row of strays, a grey coated trader was arguing with the wife of a senator.

"Of course they are clean," hissed the trader in a cross voice.

"Look under his collar!" advised an ancient female in a jewel studded collar. "That's where all the fleas are hiding."

"Madam," protested the trader in a

voice as smooth as fresh cream, "none of my strays have got fleas. It is against the law to sell strays with fleas. I don't want to lose my licence."

The Senator's wife did not look so sure. She moved along the line examining the cats. Each stray had a scroll hanging from his or her collar. On the scroll was the cat's name, their age and the country where they had been captured.

"Furia?" asked the Senator's wife. "What sort of a name is that? She looks awfully bad tempered."

"It's pronounced 'Furr-ia' – like furry," explained the trader. "She's very friendly."

"Friendly?" sneered a voice from the crowd. "She's a runner if ever I saw one. She'll be off before sunrise, unless you chain her up and beat her twice a week."

Furia's eyes were burning like lava, but she kept her mouth shut.

"Friends! Romans! You lot!" called the trader, "it's time to start the sale."

The trader's assistant banged a gong. Most of the crowd fell silent, except for a couple of gingers who were arguing about the price of fish.

"What am I bid for this fine stray? He goes by the name of Germanipuss. He's as strong as a bear this one. He was captured in the murky mountains of Maul," explained the stray-seller.

He poked Germanipuss with a stick. The big cat moved forward and turned around in a circle, opening his mouth to show off his yellow teeth.

The bidding was over quite quickly. I don't remember how much Germanipuss was sold for. I only had eyes for Furia. When she saw me, her face softened and she stopped glaring. I held up the leather bag containing my life's savings.

"Don't worry!" I yelled. "I've got my money!"

"Sold!" cried the trader. He banged the gong and pointed in my direction. My heart sank. For one horrible moment, I thought I had bought the wrong stray by accident. But it was all right, he wasn't pointing at me. Furia was the next cat up for sale.

"This little beauty has been attracting a lot of interest," said the seller, in a voice like warm olive oil. "Her name is Furia. She was captured in Hisspania. As you can see she is in excellent condition. There's not a single mark on her glossy black coat."

"Captured in Hisspania?" called a deep voice. "She's a fighter then."

"No!" laughed the trader. "She's friendly and beautifully trained."

"Why is she wearing an armoured collar?" demanded the voice. Later, I found out that the cat asking the question was called Wulfren. And if you could have seen the size of him, you'd understand why the other cats answered as soon as he asked a question.

"That's not armour, that's jewellery," said the trader nervously.

And before another question was asked, his assistant banged the gong to start the sale. Well diary, as you know, I have excellent hearing. Father used to say that with my ears I could hear a sparrow sneeze in the next village.

"What is it Father Felinious? What's wrong?" asked Wulfren.

An old voice at the back whispered:

"Nothing is wrong Wulfren. When you are as old as me, sometimes your memory plays tricks on you."

The old cat had a haunted look in his steely blue eyes.

"Can she fight Wulfren?" he asked.

"She can fight," answered Wulfren. "Look at the way she stands."

"Who will bid first?" asked the trader.

My tail flicked nervously as I padded forward and raised my paw.

"Let's start with two," I said, remembering that you had to start low. The seller nodded, looking pleased.

"Three!" boomed Wulfren. There were gasps and hisses from the crowd. I heard someone say that I was as mad as Catligula to pay that much for a stray from Hisspania.

Furia looked at me, her face was completely still.

"Four!" I called.

Wulfren hissed angrily.

"Four?" asked the auctioneer in a surprised voice. He was wondering if I was good for the money.

"In silver," I called hurriedly. "Look! I've got my money right here."

Furia caught my gaze. I'm not sure, but I think she actually smiled at me.

Wulfren growled like a wounded beast

and shook his head.

The seller nodded. His gong rang out again. I had triumphed. Furia was mine.

My Big Mistake

Feeling like the King of the Kitons, I padded up to the stray seller. My paw went to my money bag. I took a deep breath and kissed the worn leather.

"What are you doing?" asked the trader.

"Kissing goodbye to my life's savings!" I said.

"Oh yes, it's the new owner of Furia," he laughed. "Congratulations my friend! Fortune has spun you a good one."

"Be careful with that one. She bites!" whispered the assistant, smiling though his yellow teeth.

I would not blame Furia for biting him. How would you feel, being owned by a rat like that?

"Got your money?" asked the trader, licking his lips.

"Of course," I answered, opening the bag. "Four denarii – as agreed."

The assistant sniggered. The trader

smiled the very slightest of smiles.

"Who says that gingers don't have a sense of humour? Four denarii indeed!"

Silence fell like the first snows in winter.

"Four denarii. That was the price we agreed," I said flatly.

The oil had drained from the trader's voice. Now it was as cold and hard as a slab of marble.

"Four thousand denarii!" yelled the trader. "That's four THOUSAND silver coins, not four!!"

His assistant was so surprised that he dropped his gong.

How I Paid The Price

Mother told me it is wrong to laugh at older cats when they get angry. Now I understand why. The trader's paw went to the knife at his belt.

"Four denarii!' he spat. "It costs more than that to feed her for a week!"

"I'm sorry," I said with regret. "If she really costs four thousand then I'm afraid the sale is off."

With sadness rising in my heart, I turned

and padded slowly away.

"Off? Off?" spat the stray trader, his fur standing on end as he bristled with rage. "Do you think you can walk away from a deal? You might get away with that sort of trick where you come from but not in Rome!"

"I'll have to walk away," I said sadly. "I don't have that kind of money."

"Thief!" yelled the trader. "Call the guards! Send for the Watch! There's a thief in our market!"

The trader spat insults at me. An angry crowd gathered around us. My heart thundered in my chest. My fur began to bristle and stand on end. I let out a low yowl and backed away. Then a voice called:

"Stop in the name of the Emperor!"

I could see by the guard's collar that he was a Scenturian. I felt sick. My heart tried to claw its way out of my chest. Mother had warned me about the Watch. They'll lock you up in a cage for weeks if you so much as hiss at them.

The trader told his side of the story. By the time he had finished, the officer had made up his mind.

"You're under arrest," he said.

"No!" I moaned. "It's all a mistake..."

"Silence!" he growled. "You've broken Roman law. You made a false bid and cost this trader a sale. The fine is ten silver denarii or a month in prison."

"But I only have four denarii. It's all the money I have in the world," I moaned.

"Let him go Scenturian," said a voice. "If he comes with me, I will pay his fine."

It was the battered old cat who had bid against me for Furia.

"Do you agree?" asked the Scenturian.

I thought for a moment. Mother warned me never to go off with strangers.

"Well?"said the Scenturian. "Are you coming with me to prison? Or are you going with him? Choose wisely. But choose quickly. You're holding up my lunch. It's roasted cod today."

So I turned and padded off behind the old cat with the steely grey eyes.

My Debt Is Paid

"Thank you sir," I said gratefully.

He nodded and smiled a crooked smile.

He was a battered old thing but I would not like to have strayed into his territory when he was young.

"Save your thanks till we reach my school," he said. "My name is Felinious but at school they call me 'The Father'."

"School? What school is that?" I asked. He didn't look like a teacher.

"The School for Strays," he laughed. "Your lessons will begin at sunrise."

"Listen," I said. "I can pay you back..."

I was about to tell him to take me back to mother there and then. But something stopped me. On the cart there was a wooden cage. Inside that cage was the last cat in the world I'd expected to see.

"Furia!!!" I gasped. "What are you doing here?"

"Sipping cream with Queen Cleocatra!" she hissed. "What do you think I'm doing here?"

I didn't want to look stupid so I kept my mouth shut.

"Father Felinious bought me," she said. "What happened? I saw you winning the auction."

"It was the money," I sighed. "I didn't

have enough silver."

She reached through the bars and caught hold of my collar.

"But you bid anyway?" she hissed. "I thought that you had won. I was so pleased. And then… HE came to collect me."

She let out a low hiss and glared at the Father Felinious.

"I'm sorry Furia," I said. "I would have paid any price for you…"

"Except four thousand denarii," laughed the Father. "He could not afford you my dear."

Then he beckoned to his bodyguard.

A mountain of fur began to move towards me. Wulfren, the Father's guard, is twice my size. You might say that he is built like a barn, but I don't know if they have barns in Purrmania, where he comes from. Most cats his age have torn ears and battle scars, but there was hardly a mark on him.

Wulfren was carrying an iron cage. Effortlessly, he swung it up onto the back of the cart. It was like watching a kitten twirling a toy mouse.

"Get into the cage!" he ordered.

"Me?" I gasped. "You want me to get in there?"

"You belong to the Father now,' growled Wulfren.

"Why?" asked Furia. "What did he do?"

"He's a fool. He tried to buy you for four denarii," replied Wulfren.

"You're a liar!" hissed Furia in a rage.

"It's Paws' honest truth my dear," said the Father. "He won you at the auction but he couldn't pay, so he got fined – but he couldn't afford to pay his fine either and I paid it for him. So, until he pays me back he belongs to me."

It was not hard to tell that Furia was furious. She gave me a look that would have worried a pack of wild dogs.

"I'm sure we can sort this out," I said.

"Four denarii!" she hissed. "You tried to buy ME, for just four coins?"

"Four silver coins!" I said in a wounded voice. "Back where I come from that's a lot of money. How was I to know that everything in Rome is so expensive?"

"Into the cage," ordered Wulfren. "Or you will pay dearly."

In the Land of the Kitons, we are famous for our short tempers. I could not control myself. I began to bristle – the fur on my tail stuck out like a cheap brush. I let out a hiss and shot out a claw towards his face.

Then I wished I hadn't. He picked me up by the tail and smashed me into the cage door.

"Miaooowch!" I moaned. "That hurt."

"Stop it!" spat Furia. "By the Stars of Asteria! Leave him alone or…"

Wulfren bundled me into the cage. I tried to stop him, but can a pebble stop an ocean wave? Soon I was sitting in the cage licking my sore tail.

"Save it for school," said Wulfren. And he slammed the cage door shut.

MAUIS XI

May 11th

The School For Strays

As I write, the last rays of the red sun are setting and the sky is burning like a field of stubble. There is much to tell so I must get it all down quickly in my diary.

There were many things that I wanted to know on that first night here in the School for Strays. And so much I wanted to say. Firstly, I wanted to tell Father Felinious that my mother would pay off my debt. I might not have had ten denarii on me, but mother could find the money. I should have called for the guards and demanded to see the Father. One thing stopped me. I did not want to leave before I had explained to Furia that I was sorry – about the four coins thing, I mean. How can one cat own another cat? How can you put a price in silver on a cat's life? Well even so, I expect she is worth more than four coins. She did seem to be really angry about that.

I don't remember much about that first night. It was a long journey to the school, and I fell asleep to the sound of the cart wheels hammering against the stones on the road.

The next morning, I opened my eyes to find myself in a strange basket. I'd woken up late, and I sprang down a long corridor towards the sound of excited shouts. Outside in the yard, the father was inspecting a line of new pupils. Wulfren was there, pacing up and down the line.

And guess who I was standing next to? Furia! She was ignoring me, so I didn't say anything.

This was a strange school. I was one of the youngest pupils. The others looked way too old to be at school. Maybe they were being held back because they were slow learners?

"Next!" called a grumpy looking tabby.

An old ginger cat padded up for inspection.

"Name?" demanded a tall female who

was standing at Wulfren's side.

"Pusspero Ma'am," he answered.

They were strict in this place. The teacher held a long leather whip in her paw.

"How much did we pay for this one Tigra?" asked the Father. "He's older than Krownos the Ancient."

"He used to be a soldier," explained Tigra. "He says he's low on money."

I was surprised at what happened next. Tigra passed Pusspero a wooden sword. The old soldier began to practice his blows. The sword whizzed through the air as Pusspero battled an imaginary enemy.

My ears are good, so I could hear the Father and Tigra talking quietly.

"He swears he can fight, Father."

"They can all fight. But can he win Tigra?"

"Next!" called the Father.

Tigra threw the next student a wooden sword. He span around and caught it effortlessly.

"Where did you learn to handle a gladius like that?" asked Tigra.

"The same place as him," answered the

student, pointing to the old soldier. "In the legions."

"Name?" asked the scribe at the desk.

"Maxipuss. But I fight under the name of Maxi."

"He looks like a warrior," I said to myself. But the words came out aloud.

"He's a fool," hissed a voice at my side. It was Furia.

"Why?" I whispered.

"He told them his real name. Whatever you do, don't give that information away."

"Why not?" I asked.

"When you run away, they will try to hunt you down. You need to make yourself hard to find."

"What sort of school is this?" I said under my breath.

"The School for Strays is a school for gladiators," said a cracked voice at my side. It was Pusspero, the old solider. "And listen young ones, let's have no more talk of running away..."

While we were talking, the line had moved forward. Furia was next up. Tigra, the instructor, threw Furia a gladius. As the sword spun through the air, Furia's eyes never left the instructors. She didn't try to catch the spinning weapon. She didn't move a muscle. The sword landed blade down in the sand. Furia's tail began to flick.

"Wulfren, this one is for you I think," said the Father.

Wulfren came stalking over.

"Pick up the sword," he boomed. "Show us how you fight!"

"Who said I can fight?" laughed Furia.

"Every cat fights at the School for Strays," said Wulfren.

"Not me," hissed Furia, under her breath.

"Even you my pet," said the Father softly.

"Unless you'd rather empty the litter trays," said Tigra, placing the sword in the disobedient pupil's paw.

Furia wasn't trying. She swung the sword and exchanged a few blows with Tigra. But the tall instructor soon disarmed her, sending her gladius spinning into the dust.

"Are we finished?" hissed Furia.

"Why won't you fight properly?" demanded Tigra. "What is your name?"

"Answer her!" ordered Wulfren.

"I am called Furia of Hisspania," she replied.

Just then, I remembered something. When we'd met at the market, she had said something rude to me, in Squeak. The Squeak language sounds nothing like the sing-song way that they speak in sunny Hisspania.

"Keep a better grip on your sword Hisspanian," warned Tigra. "Drop your gladius like that and you will be defeated."

As I was taking this in, a voice called: "NEXT!"

"Me?" I asked.

"You! Ginger! Step forward!" boomed Wulfren.

"Name?" he demanded.

My mouth began to move, but I remembered Furia's warning about not giving them my real name. But I could not think what name to give.

"Answer when you are spoken to!"

What seemed like an age passed before I heard myself saying...

"I fight under the name of... Son of Spartapuss."

The Father whistled through his teeth.

"Son of Spartapuss? A Spartan eh? At last we've got ourselves a real warrior eh Wulfren?"

"I'm not a Spartan. My father used to work in a spa. That's why he was called Spartapuss..."

I didn't have time to finish the sentence. The whole school broke into peels of cruel laughter. It rang around the courtyard and bounced off the stone walls. Even Wulfren was smiling.

"Hail Son of Spartapuss!" sneered a voice from the back. "His father works in a spa!"

"Silence!" hissed the Father, and the crowd went as quiet as a tomb. "Tigra, let's see if our Spartan can fight."

A wooden sword came spinning through the air towards me. Without thinking, I stuck out a paw and tried to catch it by the handle. But it bounced off my paw and crashed into the sand.

"I told you, I'm not a Spartan..." I hissed picking up the wooden sword.

"They know you are not a Spartan," whispered Furia. "They are playing with you."

The crowd clapped slowly. Tigra beckoned me forward.

"Wait!" I cried. My knees began to wobble.

"What is it?" hissed Tigra.

"Are you sure I should be fighting against a female?" I asked.

Tigra shook her head very slowly and snarled. I realised that the words that had just left my mouth were not very wise. She stood completely still, glaring at me. Then she flicked out her paw and threw her sword at me. The wooden point pinned my tail to the ground. The pain was quite bad but I managed to smile.

"You've dropped your weapon!" I said. "I thought you said we were supposed to keep hold of our swords."

I realised that this was also not a wise thing to say. "You probably meant to do that, didn't you?" I added.

"You'd fight a lot better if you talked less lad," advised Pusspero.

I extracted my tail from under Tigra's sword. Miaowch!!! It really stung.

Tigra beckoned me forward.

So I raised my gladius and charged at her. The next thing I knew, I found myself face down in the sand with Tigra's delicate claws pinning me down by my whiskers.

"Miiiaaaooowwwwch!" I moaned again. "That REALLY hurts!"

"If that's a Spartan warrior, I'm Helen of Tray!" came a shout from the back.

I wondered who the joker was.

The crowd laughed again. Looking up, I noticed that Furia was not laughing with the rest of them.

"Enough!" ordered Wulfren. "At least our Spartan showed some spirit. That's more than I can say for you, Furia."

MAUIS XII

May 12th

Queen of the Cats

Today they had us working all day, training with our weapons. The only one not joining in was Furia. When the 'doctors' (that's what they call the teachers here) were watching, Furia fought with the rest of us. But as soon as they looked away, she stopped practicing.

We didn't leave the training ground until sunset. By the time I made it down to the canteen, I was starving. As I padded in, the place was buzzing. Maxi was telling jokes, Clawdia was clipping her claws. Herc was helping himself to an extra helping from the cream bowl. There was no sign of Pusspero. I spotted Furia sitting on a bench by herself so I went to join her.

"I'll say one thing about this school. The food is excellent. And the portions are big too. Look at these dormice! Why aren't you eating Furia?"

"You wouldn't understand," she sighed.

"Try me," I said, trying not to sound hurt.

"I'm not eating because I want to look weak and out of condition," she explained.

"Why?" I asked in amazement.

"So they won't pick me to fight."

She leapt down from the bench and started to pad off.

"Why don't you want to fight? Are you afraid?" I asked.

"No," she replied. And I believed her.

"Then why?" I asked.

Her orange eyes grew wider.

"I won't fight so that they can enjoy watching me," she said. "I only fight when I have to, on the battlefield. I'm not fighting in front of a crowd of hissing idiots. And I'll never fight to make that fool Felinious rich."

"Hail Furia! The Queen of the Cats!" sneered a voice beside me. "She's too proud to fight."

It was Maxi, one of the strongest gladiators in our group.

"I'm terribly sorry your highness," he mocked. "When the Father puts you in the arena, you'll fight just like the rest of us."

Furia snatched the bowl from the table.

"Never!" she hissed.

Maxi and his friends laughed. I could tell by her fiery eyes that she was serious.

"Come on Furia, I need your help," I said, leaping down from the bench.

"What?" spat Furia. She was still looking at Maxi in the way that a hunting hawk eyes a rabbit.

I quickly grabbed a bowl, piled it up with treats and passed it to Furia.

"Come on Furia, I told Pusspero we'd take him some food," I said.

It was the truth. Pusspero was too tired to make it to the canteen. But I also wanted to get Furia away from Maxi.

I thought she was going to smash the plate into Maxi's face so I was relieved when she followed me out of the canteen towards the sleeping area.

As we left, Furia muttered something under her breath. I remembered the mystery of Furia speaking in Squeak when we first met back in the market.

"Furia, you're not really from Hisspania are you?" I asked.

"No," she said flatly. "I'm not. And if I were you, I'd get a message out to your family. Get them to pay your debt. Buy yourself out Son of Spartapuss, before it is too late."

MAUIS XIII
May 13th

Poor old Pusspero was glad of the food we took him last night. There was still no sign of him on the training field today. I hope he is all right. Wulfren had us going through our drills with the gladius. He says that he has a surprise for us tomorrow. It doesn't sound pleasant.

Meanwhile, Furia still won't train unless the instructors are standing next to her. I keep telling her that she won't get away with it but she doesn't care.

I'm still thinking about Furia's advice. What is stopping me from asking my mother to pay up and get me out of here?

MAUIS XIV

May 14th

The ground was cold under my paws as Wulfren led us through the school grounds. At last we came to a high wall made of white stone. Then I noticed the mosaic floor beneath my paws. The design showed the mouth of an enormous dog. The picture was picked out in red and black tiles. Lines of white tiles formed rows of jagged teeth.

Wulfren fumbled with a set of iron keys.

"What in Paws' name has the Wolf got planned for us now?" whispered Lucca.

He flicked his grey tail nervously.

"Wait for me!" called a voice.

Pusspero came trotting up, puffing and wheezing like a cracked kettle. His fur needed brushing and he looked totally exhausted.

"Morning grandfather," laughed Maxi. "I wanted to ask you something..."

"What is it lad?" replied Pusspero.

"Are we fighting with the wooden swords again?" asked Maxi with a wicked gleam in his eye.

Pusspero nodded. "Yes lad, we are."

"I've lost my sword. Lend me your walking stick will you?" boomed Maxi.

The old soldier glared at Maxi and began to bristle with rage.

"Walking stick? I'll stick you..." he coughed, "you flashy young flea-brain!"

Never one to back down, Maxi stepped towards Pusspero, with his claws out.

Before Pusspero could respond, Wulfren pushed at the oak door with his enormous paw. Slowly, the great wooden gate swung open.

"Students of the School for Strays, welcome to Hades' Hallway!" he boomed.

As everyone knows, Hades is the ruler of the Underworld. This didn't sound good.

I padded slowly forward into a practice arena surrounded by row upon row of wooden benches. The seats were empty. I imagined a packed house with thousands of eyes watching me. Was this why I was still here? Had I come to learn how to stand upon the sand and fight for my life? My tail began to flick.

My eyes left the rows of seats and roamed across the practice arena. In the middle of the ring was one of the strangest machines I've ever seen. It seemed to be powered by bags of sand attached to wheels, connected to a jumble of ropes and pulleys.

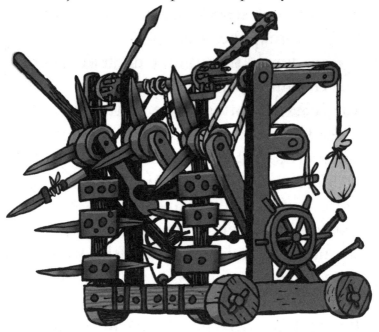

"Meet my pet, The Octopus," growled Wulfren as he stroked the curious machine lovingly with his enormous paw. "But be careful! It bites. Which one of you wants to go first?"

I can't stand long silences. I was just thinking about volunteering when I felt Pusspero's paw on my shoulder.

"Wait for it lad," he wheezed.

"I'll try!" called Herc. "Go first and get it over with. That's what my old dad used to say."

He padded through the ranks to the front, until he stood about a tail length away from the machine.

"Mind you... that didn't do him much good. Got himself killed in the first minute of the siege of Cattage," he muttered.

I like Herc but he is a nervous talker.

"Get ready!" ordered Wulfren, grabbing throwing Herc a wooden sword.

Herc gripped the gladius.

"Defend yourself!" warned Wulfren as he turned a wooden wheel at the side of the machine.

With a clattering noise the Octopus jerked into action. The paddles lifted. Bags of sand rose and fell. The wheels began to turn and the machine crawled slowly forwards like a great wooden beetle. Rows of wooden swords rose and fell, swishing through the air as they advanced towards poor Hercatules.

Herc began to block the blows, keeping his fighting stance as the machine built up speed.

"Go on Hercatules!" called a voice from the crowd. "Cut its arms off!"

Herc's ear twitched back ever so slightly as he heard the shout. And that was his downfall. Wulfren pulled on the rope, slowing the attacking blades for a moment. Herc's sword went out to block a blade that was no longer there. With a crash, the wooden sword smacked into his chest and knocked him flying. He landed with a heavy thud, face down in the sand.

"Can I have another go?" he moaned.

"Silence!" growled Wulfren. "You're dead. The dead don't talk. Who is next?"

No one raised their paw.

"How about you Hisspanian?"

Furia had not spoken a single word to anyone that morning and she wasn't going to start now. She glared at the instructor silently, flicking her tail slowly against the sand.

"Pick Pusspero!" called a voice from the back. "We need an experienced soldier to show the rest of us how this is done."

"Who said that?" growled Tigra.

The head instructor had come to watch the students work. "No more calling out.

You are here to learn, not to wail and mew like fish sellers!"

"Come on... who is next?" demanded Wulfren.

I could not believe what I saw next. Hissero and Cato, two of Maxi's friends, were standing behind Pusspero. The pair of them shoved him in the back, pushing him out of the ranks. He let out an angry hiss.

"Pusspero? Very well!" said Tigra.

Wulfren let go of the rope.

"Defend yourself," he called.

The wooden machine jerked into action once again. Wheels turned, levers lifted and ropes whizzed over cogs. Soon the rows of wooden swords were rising and falling again. Unstoppable, the machine crawled towards Pusspero. He swung his gladius left and right, blocking each blow as the blades whizzed past his whiskers. Pusspero was fighting well, but he started to weaken. As the machine built up speed, he seemed to shrink into himself.

Then Wulfren suddenly pulled on a rope to delay the striking swords. It was the same move that had defeated Herc earlier.

The old solider nearly fell for it, but at the last moment he held back his strike and waited. Then he neatly brought his gladius back up to block a combination of hammering sword swipes.

"Watch him!" called Tigra "Learn from his technique. His eyes never lost sight of the blades. That's why he lasted for so many years in the army. He's a survivor."

"Old Krownus?" laughed Maxi, pointing at Pusspero. "He was just lucky."

"That old fleabag wouldn't last five minutes in the arena," called another voice. "My grandmother hits harder than that."

"Silence!" ordered Tigra.

Wulfren turned the wheel. Slowly, the machine came to a standstill.

"Why stop now when we're having fun?" laughed Maxi.

"Father Felinious, salve!" said Tigra politely. (Salve is the Catin word for hello!)

"Get them working in pairs please Tigra," ordered Father Felinious. "We have a guest coming to watch tomorrow."

"Pairs it is Father," said the instructor.

MAUIS XVI

May 16th

Flea Hundred

Tonight everyone was talking about the rich visitor with the golden collar who came to watch us. This morning they woke us up earlier than usual. We were given clean costumes and school collars. They even gave us a brushing. Soon we were waiting patiently for our instructors to put us into pairs.

One by one, the others were picked. When Clawdia was paired with Pusspero, Maxi let out a hiss.

"Hey Clawdia," he laughed. "If you want a quick win, throw a cushion onto the sand. Old cats like Krownus over there can't resist a lie down on a soft cushion."

Before Pusspero could reply, I heard Maxi shouting at me.

"Hey you! Flea Hundred!!!"

"What's he on about now?" I groaned.

"He means the Three Hundred," said Herc. "You know, the famous three hundred SPARTAN warriors who fought at the battle of Furmopolae..."

"Oh!" I groaned. "And why does he keep calling Pusspero 'Krownus'?"

"Krownus is the Squeak God of Time. He's the oldest god on Mount Olympuss. You ought to know that partner," laughed a familiar voice.

I could not believe my bad fortune. I'd been paired up with Maxipuss. This was unlucky for two reasons. Firstly, he was annoying. Secondly, he treated every practice as if it was a fight to the death.

"You're going down Spartan!" he called.

"I'm not a Spartan..." I replied.

"He knows," said Herc.

"He's only winding you up lad," added Pusspero.

Tigra gave out some wooden swords. Soon we were trading blows.

"Keep those blades up!" ordered Wulfren.

"You heard him Spartan," echoed Maxi. "Keep the tip of your gladius up!"

"For Peus' sake! Stop calling me 'Spartan!' I am not a Spartan!" I hissed.

Before the words were out of my mouth, Maxi's blade came flashing past my ear.

"No talking while you fight," ordered

Tigra. "The Father is here."

Father Felinious was leading a proud looking guest to a special place in the front row. A special purple cushion had been put down to make her comfortable.

"Just look at them," said the Father. "Each one is a peach. Every fighting cat here has been picked by me. Each one is as sharp as Paws' claws. It's impossible to choose between them..."

The guest silenced the Father with the wave of her paw.

"Enough of your market patter Felinious. It will not work on me," she snapped.

"Who is she?" I asked.

"That's Purrgusta, the Senator's wife" said Lucca, who was fighting alongside us. "Everyone knows her. Her parties are the talk of Rome."

"They don't throw parties in Sparta," laughed Maxi. "They throw their unwanted kittens off cliffs!"

While he was laughing at his own joke, I landed a blow on his sword arm, and he let out a mew of pain.

"I'm not a Spartan!" I growled.

"Faster pussycats!" ordered Tigra. "Our

honourable visitor wants to see you fight like lions!"

"What's a Roman noble like Purrgusta doing here?" I asked.

"Probably looking for entertainment," said Herc.

"She won't find much entertainment around here," I said, blocking another blow.

"We are the entertainment," yelled Maxi. "You Spartan flea-wit!"

As he shouted, he took a sneaky swipe at my legs but I side-stepped it.

"Here they come. Let's make it look good!" said Maxi, putting in some more effort and picking up the pace. I did my best to respond, blocking his blows as well as I could.

"Don't make it look TOO good lad," wheezed a voice at my side. It was Pusspero.

"Why not?" I asked, stepping back as Maxi thrust forwards.

"Don't get yourself picked..." he gasped. But he was struggling to breathe. Noticing him in trouble, Furia slowed her attack and began to circle slowly. She raised her net and shifted her trident from paw to paw. Anyone watching would think that she was preparing to strike, but I knew that she was giving our friend the chance to get his breath back.

"Are these your best fighters Felinious?" asked Purrgusta. "They look weak to me."

"Weak?" gasped Felinious. "These are the finest gladiators in the Feline Empire."

"That pair might do," said Purrgusta. "The big one is good, but he's a bit over weight. And the ginger one is clumsy."

They were talking about Maxi and me.

"They call him 'The Spartan'," said the

Father. "I captured him myself in the dark Forests of Purrmania. He is a specialist with the gladius."

"There were no Spartans in the forests of Purrmania," sighed the Senator's wife. "Every young kitten knows that Sparta is in the Land of the Squeaks."

"I can explain that..." began the Father. "He was in the forest, on his way to his grandmother's house..."

The Senator's wife had the quicker tongue.

"Nonsense! Besides, the Spartans did not fight with swords, they used spears," she hissed.

Felinious forced himself to smile.

"Some Spartans used swords, I believe..." he began.

"And history does not record that the Spartans were gingers," she growled. "Really Felinious, do you take me for a total fool? I need proper gladiators for my party. My husband wants to put on a good show for the Ambassador of Cattage."

But before I could hear any more, the Father and his knowledgeable guest moved on to inspect the others.

MAUIS XVII
May 17th

This morning I woke up to a row. The whole of the School for Strays was buzzing with excited voices.

"Spartan! Wake up!" boomed Maxi.

My paws ached. My back ached. My claws ached. Every part of me was as stiff as a badger's bristles.

"What's the matter?" I moaned, poking my nose out of my basket.

"Wolfy wants us," gasped Maxipuss. "You know what that means?"

"What?" I asked.

I am not at my best when I have just woken up.

"We've been picked!" he was shaking with excitement.

"Just you and me?" I asked.

"No. There are four of us. Three to fight and one spare, for back up."

"Come on!" he called, shaking my basket. "You've already missed your breakfast, but I brought you this."

He put a delicious looking bowl of baked fish in front of me.

"Thanks Maxi," I began sniffing the bowl carefully.

"Eat up," he said. "Cod in jelly is good for your strength."

I looked into his eyes.

"Why are you suddenly being so friendly? Yesterday you were insulting me."

Maxi laughed and slapped me on the shoulder. '"Yesterday was different Spartan," he said.

But this time there was no sneer in his voice as he said the nickname. "Now we are on the same team. We must be strong, if we are to beat the team from Cattage."

The news went around the school like a flea epidemic but we heard the full story first from Wulfren. Our visitor's husband, a senator, was giving a party for the Ambassador of Cattage. The Ambassador loves sports – so much that he has brought his favourite gladiators with him, to fight against a team of Romans.

As I explained this to Herc, Furia bristled.

"But I still don't understand it," said Herc. "Maxi is a strong fighter. Everyone thought that he would get picked. But

Pusspero is old. And Furia says that she won't fight. And you..."

"What about me?" I asked.

"Well Spartan..." said Herc. "You are hardly top of the class. You've never even been to the arena before."

My tail began to flick.

"Why would the Father pick a team like that?" he asked.

"Maybe he wants you to lose!" called a voice from behind me.

"Lose?" I gasped. "Whatever makes you think that he wants us to lose!"

When I turned around, she was gone.

I sprang after her but she was already racing off down the corridor. Her paws made no sound against the mosaic floor. For a moment, I thought that I wasn't going to be able to catch her. Then a guard came by and Furia had to stop in her tracks while she waited for the danger to pass.

Making as little noise as possible, I padded up beside her.

"Furia!" I whispered. "What are you doing?"

"What does it look like?" she hissed.

"If you're running away," I whispered,

"I'm not here to stop you."

"Good," she replied. "You won't change my mind."

She stroked an object on her collar. I noticed that she was wearing a golden charm, shaped like a wheel.

"What did you mean just then?" I asked. "About the Father wanting our team to lose against the fighters from Cattage."

Her amber eyes flashed in the sun.

"I meant exactly what I said," she laughed. "The Senator wants to keep the Ambassador happy. I expect she's asked Felinious to pick a team that will lose."

I thought about it for a moment.

"You mean cheat? Fix a gladiator contest? The Father would never do that!"

Furia's tail began to flick impatiently. If it hadn't been for the danger of being spotted by the guards on the watch tower, she would have been off and away without saying another word. But instead she whispered:

"Where in the wide world did you grow up? Of course he would cheat. That old rat would do anything to make a profit."

She sniffed the air for the scent of the

guards.

"Well, Son of Spartapuss, I won't fight for the Father. You should buy yourself out, while you still can!"

With these words she sprang towards the wall like a rat up a pipe.

The school wall is twenty tails high and covered in sharp thorns. Suddenly I heard voices from the watchtower. Guards wait in the tower, on the look out for students trying to escape. I turned around to see what the noise was. When I looked again, Furia had vanished into the misty evening.

As I padded back towards the canteen, a hundred questions ran through my head.

Before I could work out any answers, Maxi appeared.

"There you are!" called Maxi. "I've been searching for you everywhere. Tigra wants to see us right now. It's about the match tomorrow."

Ten minutes later, Maxi, Pusspero and I were called into Tigra's rooms. We already knew that it was a demonstration match. Our team was representing Rome. We would be up against the Ambassador's fighters, from Cattage.

Tigra explained that each team would have three gladiators and a spare. She used strange names like 'Purmillo', 'Net-cat' and 'Furacian'. These names meant nothing to me at the time. Later I found out that they are names for different types of gladiators.

We were going to be fighting with metal weapons but our sword points and claws were to be covered. It was not a death match. When Tigra explained this last part, Wulfren looked a little bit disappointed.

"Any questions?" she asked.

I remembered what Furia had said and I raised my paw.

"Will it be a fair fight?" I asked.

Wulfren hissed and lumbered towards me. He looked even bigger close up, like a tower covered in fur.

"What do you mean by that Spartan?" he demanded.

"Er... nothing," I answered quickly.

He let out a low growl. It was the kind of noise that a wolf makes if you take away its dinner.

"The Spartan wants to know if it will be a fair fight," he said. "Well, remember this, all of you, because it might save your lives. There is no such thing as a fair fight. So when those beasts from Cattage come at you, you'd better make sure that you're ready for anything."

MAUIS XVIII

May 18th

Yesterday passed quickly, with hours of hard training. Tigra had us dodging spear thrusts and practising our blocking moves. When night fell, I slept like a bear in winter.

The next morning, she led us to a special practice session.

There was no sign of Furia. I could not understand it. Surely someone must have noticed that she was missing? Her name was on the list along with ours.

As the day of the match drew nearer, we started to pay attention. Tigra gave me a large golden helmet shaped like the head of a fish. I put it on. It was heavy. I found it hard to see anything because the slits over the eyes were too narrow.

"Thanks, but I think I'd fight better without this," I said, struggling to get the helmet off.

"Leave it on," ordered Tigra.

Before I could protest, she explained.

"You are our Purmillo, so you have to wear that fish helmet. It's traditional."

She took away my sword and gave me a small knife.

"For Peus' sake!" I moaned. "What's this supposed to be?"

"That's your weapon," she answered. "Purmillos wear a helmet and fight with a dagger."

I knew that I was going to risk my life

but no one had told me that I had to wear a helmet shaped like a fish while I was doing it! Tigra saw me hesitating.

"It's a Roman joke. You will fight against the Net-cat with his fishing spear (the trident). So it's a cat fighting a fish! If the cat gets killed by the fish, the crowd think it's funny. Get it now?" she asked.

"Er... maybe." I muttered. "Can I have my sword back?"

How in Paws' name was I supposed to beat a trident with a silly little dagger the size of a dinner knife?

Maxi was delighted with his weapons. He'd been chosen as our 'Furacian'. That meant that he got to fight with a sword. He also had a helmet, but his had a wide metal brim. On his left paw, he held a tiny shield. It didn't give much protection, but it was better than nothing.

"Where's our Net-cat?" asked Maxi.

"Here!" croaked Pusspero.

"You?" gasped a surprised Maxi.

"Yeah, me!" hissed Pusspero.

"Got a problem with that?" asked Tigra.

"No. But... he's an ex-soldier, like me. The Roman army never fight with spears. Spears are for savages, that's what we used to say. Where's Furia? Her tribe are experts with the spear."

"Good question," growled Wulfren. "Where is Furia?"

"We know you don't want to tell tales," said Tigra. "But the Father will track her down. He always finds runaways, as sure as night follows day. If you help us find her before the match, it will be better for her. Her punishment won't be as... harsh."

The three of us studied each other's eyes. Wulfren glared at me but I kept silent. I wasn't going to tell what I knew.

"What's in it for us if we tell you?" asked Maxi.

"Think about this," said Wulfren, "if Furia fights with you, you might not lose."

MAUIS XIX

May 19th

Rome Vs Cattage

That night I hardly slept a wink. I wanted to taste the night air, but when I tried the door of my room it was locked. The Father wasn't taking any chances. When morning finally came they woke us later than usual. Soon we were eating a breakfast of champions. Then they sent us back to our rooms for a rest. The same thing happened at lunchtime. By the time they finally came to call for us, the setting sun was turning the clouds the colour of a fine red wine.

At last I stood waiting outside the gate of the School for Strays.

"Are you scared lad?" asked Pusspero.

"No," I lied. Tigra had made me practice again and again, but I still didn't feel confident fighting with the knife.

"A little grain of fear is good for you," said Pusspero. "They say that an oyster needs a grain of sand to make a pearl."

Pusspero had a lot of sayings like this. I always nodded when he came out with them. But I could not see how fear could help me to fight with a silly little dagger.

Suddenly a cart came into view. Driving the cart was the bulky figure of Wulfren. On the back of the cart was a large cage. Inside was a tall figure wearing a Purmillo style helmet. I noticed that this cat was chained to the bars of the cage.

"Get in," ordered Wulfren. "The team from Cattage are waiting."

We leapt into the cage. I wasn't best pleased when he chained me to the bars.

"Morning friend. Are you fighting today?" asked Pusspero. But there was no reply from behind the bronze visor.

"Suit yourself," said Maxi. "Let your gladius do the talking eh?"

The figure in the helmet sat as still as a heron on a riverbank. I wondered if he could understand the Catin language. Gladiators come from every corner of the Feline Empire. Not all of them speak Catin.

"Where's the Father?" I asked. "I thought he always comes to watch his fighters."

"He always comes to collect his money more like," said Pusspero, with a cough.

"He's probably at the villa already," said Maxi.

"Villa?" I asked. "Aren't we going to fight in an arena?"

Pusspero shook his head.

"You Spartan half wit!" laughed Maxi. "We're fighting at the Senator's villa, not the Coliseum!"

"He's right," said Pusspero with a grim smile. "The guests will stuff their faces and chat about our deaths afterwards..."

"I thought they said it wasn't a death match," I whispered in shaky voice.

Pusspero did not answer. He started to cough. It was a rattling, choking cough that left him struggling to breathe.

"Fur ball!" laughed Maxi. "Cough it up. Better out than in!"

The cart bumped to a halt. At first I

thought it was another traffic jam.

"Get out!" boomed Wulfren, appearing with a bag of equipment slung over his mountainous shoulder. He opened the cage and unchained us. Now we could move freely. All except our new friend in the helmet, who was led out on a short lead.

As we waited at the gates of a villa, a young tabby padded up. She noticed the blade of my dagger sticking out of Wulfren's bag.

"Are you the knife sharpeners?" she asked. "We don't need any knives sharpening today."

"We're gladiators Ma'am. We're here for Purrgusta's party," explained Wulfren.

"Gladiators?" said the tabby in a surprised voice. "Sorry, you don't look much like gladiators. Besides, the gladiators are here already."

"That's probably the team from Cattage," said Maxi. "We're the team from Rome. They call me Maxi. My real name is Maxipuss, but Maxi is easier for the fans to shout."

The little tabby frowned.

"May mighty Paws protect you!" she

said. Then she led us inside. "Hurry up! The party has already started."

The villa was a vision in marble. Every time you put your paw down, it landed on an expensive mosaic.

"This lot are rolling in riches," said Maxi. "I bet they've even got a mosaic in their vomitorium."

"Of course they are rich. He's a senator..." began Pusspero. But his words ended in another bout of coughing. Poor Pusspero was determined to finish his sentence. When he'd got his breath back he added:

"You need over one million denarii before they... let you... become a senator."

"No more chatter," ordered Wulfren. "Save your breath for the fight."

The tabby led us into a large courtyard.

As we padded across, I could smell roasting cod and fried oysters. Music floated through the night air. There was a drummer, a trumpeter and a lyre player. The drummer pounded out a lazy beat. But that lyre cat really knew his way around his instrument. I was watching his paws dancing up and down the fretboard when

I heard Maxi's voice shouting.

"Look!!!" he gasped. "Look over there Spartan!"

One half of the courtyard had been set out like an arena. There was a sandy floor and banks of cushioned seats where the guests were waiting. Maxi was not looking at the seats. He had just caught sight of the team from Cattage.

There was only one word for the team from Cattage: champions. Their smallest fighter was easily bigger than Maxi. Their biggest was a giant. He towered over Wulfren. Their coats shone in the torchlight. Their eyes were as bright as their spear tips. Their collars were made of gold and set with precious rubies and emeralds. They looked like winners.

"Paws help us!" I hissed. "Look at the size of that one. He's enormous. I've seen smaller lions!"

Maxi had lost a little of his swagger.

"They look very... professional," he said. His tail began to flick nervously. "Look at their weapons. They shine like the summer sun."

Only Pusspero didn't seem too bothered.

"It is said that the dirty sword can still cut clean," he said with a cough.

This was another of Pusspero's sayings. I was not so sure about it. If you have got a dirty sword, it stands to reason that you probably don't sharpen it much. I wondered if he had any sayings about how to fight a giant with a dagger. I was just about to ask when I heard a loud blast on the trumpet.

"Ambassador! Senator! Honoured Guests! May I have your attention. Please take your places, tonight's Games are about to begin."

It was Father Felinious. When he had finished talking, he called us over with a wave of his wooden sword.

"What's he doing with that?" I asked. "I thought we were supposed to be fighting with real weapons."

"Spartan, you really do have ginger fluff for brains sometimes," laughed Maxi.

"The wooden sword is the symbol of a gladiator who has won his freedom," explained Wulfren.

"Was Father Felinious a gladiator?" I asked.

Wulfren didn't answer. He led us over to where the Father was waiting. I noticed that he was talking to someone. It was the gladiator in the helmet who had come in the cart with us.

"Do you still refuse to fight?" hissed the Father.

The gladiator in the helmet nodded.

"You'll regret this!" growled the Father.

Wulfren passed me my Purmillo helmet.

"Where's my dagger," I asked.

"Not yet," said Wulfren.

Later, I learned that gladiators are never given their weapons until they are standing in the ring. There was no point in arguing, so I put on the silly fish head helmet.

The drums began to beat. The band struck up with a tune called the *March of the Gladiators*. A couple of the guests clapped as Maxi, Pusspero and I padded into the ring and began to parade around.

"Ambassador! Senator! Honoured Guests! I give you... Rome's finest gladiators. The School for Strays!" announced Father Felinious, waving his wooden sword in the air.

I waited for the roar of the crowd, but there was no roar. Most of the guests weren't even looking at us. I heard one of them complaining that his cream tasted sour, as if it had been left out in the sun. This cut me like a sword stroke.

"Why aren't they watching us?" I asked.

"You have to... make them watch. Win their eyes. It is said..." began Pusspero. But his sentence ended in a hacking cough.

Suddenly the drums began to beat louder

and the trumpet sounded.

"And for their opponents today I give you... The pride of Africanus. The undefeated Lions of Cattage!"

There was a loud cheer from the crowd.

"Undefeated?" moaned Maxi. "Undefeatable more like!"

When we'd finished our lap, we left the ring.

"Can I take this helmet off? It's as hot as Hades' kettle in here," I gasped.

Wulfren helped me to get the heavy helmet off. As I removed my fish head, two faces in the crowd caught my eye.

The first cat was enormously fat and his golden collar was dotted with sparkling jewels. This was the Ambassador from Cattage. Everything here at the party: the music; the fine food and the gladiator games had been put on to impress him. With my helmet off, I could easily hear their conversation.

"Still fancy your chances Senator?" he yowled. "I think my brave lions are about to eat your Roman goats."

"We are all Romans now," said the Senator. Back in his grandfather's time, Rome had defeated Cattage in battle. It had belonged to Rome ever since.

"Let us make this a little more interesting," growled the Ambassador.

The Senator tried not to groan. He was as thin as a spear. He looked as if a strong gust of wind would blow him over. He had held many parties like this before. I knew what he was thinking. If someone at a party says: "Let us make this a little more interesting," it can only mean one thing: a bet.

"I will make it easy for you," said the Ambassador. "I will let two of your Roman fighters go against one of my lions."

The Senator smiled. He didn't want to say "yes" too quickly. He had put aside five hundred denarii for tonight. He knew he was going to lose it and he didn't mind. The Emperor wanted the Ambassador to be happy. He wasn't going to be happy unless he won some gold.

"Are you sure?" said the Senator, pretending to hesitate. "One of yours against two Romans?"

"Two against one. That's what I just said," laughed the Ambassador. "I bet one hundred silver coins. Cattage will beat Rome!"

"I accept the bet. But you can pick the fighters," purred the Senator.

Just then I felt the thud of Wulfren's heavy paw on my shoulder.

"Spartan, you and Maxi get ready," he ordered. He helped me as I struggled to stuff my head into the helmet again.

Wulfren led us to the edge of the ring, and only then did he give us our weapons. Maxi lashed his small shield to one arm and practiced a few swipes of the sword.

"Fight bravely Spartan!" he said. He

thumped the top of my helmet with his sword. This was really annoying. I didn't need Maxi to tell me to fight bravely. Besides, it was all right for him. I only had a dagger to defend myself with.

"See the giant? He's mine!" hissed Maxi.

"Which giant?" I replied.

They were all giants.

"It's going to be the two of us against one of them," I whispered. I'd just over-heard the Ambassador talking about it.

The war horn sounded and the drums began to beat as we entered the ring.

We looked up at the Lions of Cattage. They glared proudly back at us.

"Friends! Senator! Ambassador! Fighting for the honour of Rome tonight, I present Maxipuss the Mighty..."

I thought it could not get any worse, but it just did. Win or lose, Maxi was going to be even more unbearable now he'd been given the name: Maxipuss the Mighty.

"...and fighting alongside him, for the first time, let me present the mysterious new fighter known as The Spartan."

"Raise your weapon when they say your name," hissed Maxi.

"I'm not a Spartan! How many times do I have to keep telling you!" I moaned.

"You are now," said Maxi snatching my paw and raising it up into the air.

There were a few cheers from the crowd.

"Cattage must be destroyed!" called a voice. I think it was a cook that Maxi had been talking to earlier.

"And going up against our two Roman fighters tonight, we have the Pride of Cattage. The undefeated champion. The fearsome... Fish-Eater."

"Why is he called the Fish-Eater?" I asked. "Is he on a special diet or something?"

"He's their Net-Cat," said Maxi. "That means he fights Purmillos. So you'd better watch out fish-face!"

Maxi bashed the blunt end of his sword down on my fish-shaped helmet. Before I could get him back, the fighter from Cattage padded forward. I was glad that it was not the giant. But the one who came towards me was twice my size at least. In his paw he held a long trident. And over his shoulder was a fishing net.

The crowd went wild and began to cheer.

I guess it was because they were impressed with the bravery of a fighter who would go up against two. Or perhaps they had been paid to cheer.

"Cattage! Cattage!" roared the crowd.

"Let's take him down Spartan," hissed Maxi. "That will shut them up."

The Fish-Eater stepped forward and began to circle. I held back as Maxi sprang forward, aiming a blow at our opponent's throat. As quick as a whip, the fighter from Cattage blocked it with his trident. Then his other paw flicked and the net dropped from his shoulder.

"Come here little fish!" he hissed.

When I realised he was talking to me I felt a bit weak. My heart started to beat faster and faster.

"Cattage! Cattage! Cattage!" cheered the crowd.

I couldn't help it, I started to back away.

"Stand your ground," warned Maxi.

"That's easy for you to say!" I moaned.

Maxi leapt forward and swung his gladius towards the wooden shaft of the trident. But the wood was strong. The spear did not snap in half when the sword connected with it. The Fish-Eater let out a little mew of delight. He stuck out his paw again and I saw the trident coming straight for my eyes. Instinctively, I threw my head forward. There was a deafening clang as the three pointed spear struck my face. My helmet might look stupid, but it had just saved my life.

Maxi saw his chance. With the trident out of range, he struck a blow for the Roman team. It landed on the Fish-Eater's paw and he dropped his net, wincing in pain. As fast as a lightening bolt from Mewpiter, he tried to snatch it back up. I sprang forward and rolled. The trident smashed into the sand by my face. Somehow, I managed to grab the net and sweep it away from the Fish-Eater's searching paw.

The crowd gasped.

"Nice roll!" yelled Maxi. "You're braver than you look Spartan."

When I raised the net I heard shouts from the crowd.

"What shall I do with this?" I asked as I twirled the net through the air.

"Wait! Don't throw it! You'll miss and he'll take it back from you," cried Maxi.

The fighter from Cattage let out a hiss. He'd lost his net but he still had his trident.

"Who's first you Roman rats?" he spat, raising the three-pronged spear.

Maxi sprang forward. The Fish-Eater dodged the attack and came at me. The trident smashed against my helmet again. This time I lost my balance and I fell sprawling into the sand. I heard the clang of Maxi's sword as it connected with the tip of the trident.

"Net him Spartan! Do it now!" hissed Maxi.

I drew back my arm and let go. The net went spinning through the air. Fortune was with me, because it fell straight over the Fish-eater's head. Maxi saw his chance. He lunged forwards and landed on top of his back with dull thud.

"Catch me now, fish breath!" he laughed.

The Fish-Eater let out a wounded yowl as I leapt over and grabbed the trident from his shaking paw. Tangled up in his own net, and with Maxi on top of him, the Fish-Eater had nowhere to go.

"Eat sand, fish face!" laughed Maxi, rubbing his enemy's nose into the sand.

The Fish-Eater dragged his claw through the dust three times, the sign that he had given up the fight. It was not a pretty victory, but I had won my first match.

As I took off my helmet, I heard the Senator apologising.

"Bad luck Ambassador! Your Fish-Eater fought with skill," he said politely.

"Clumsy fool! I will feed him to the fishes!" hissed the Ambassador.

"Come now," said the Senator. "Let's watch another bout. This time we will keep it simple. One of yours will fight against one of ours."

"Alright," agreed the Ambassador, brightening up at the thought of winning his money back. "But you can pick the fighters this time. I insist!"

"What's going on?" I asked as I padded slowly back to our area at the side of the ring.

"It's going to be one of their lot versus one of us," said Maxi.

"Who are Cattage sending out next?" I asked.

I followed Maxi's eyes towards where the Cattage team were waiting.

"Paws' Claws!" I said. "Who are they sending against that monster?"

I hoped it wasn't me.

Maxi pointed at Pusspero.

"Pusspero?" I gasped. "But he's too ill to fight. That beast will batter him."

"When you're picked, you're picked," said Pusspero, struggling bravely from his seat.

"Sit down!" I said, pushing him back

to the bench. At that moment Wulfren's long shadow fell over us.

"Come on Pusspero," said Wulfren.

"He's too sick to go out there," said Maxi. "Let me go instead."

Wulfren let out a grunt and stalked off towards the Father. We waited in silence. At last he came back with the answer.

"The Father says no," said the big instructor.

"Why can't I take his place?" groaned Maxi.

"The Ambassador wants to watch new fighters," he sighed.

"Ask him again," I begged. "Please!"

Wulfren hissed and muttered a curse under his breath. Then he lumbered off to speak to the Father again. As soon as Wulfren had left, Maxi turned to the stranger in the helmet who had been sitting quietly through all of this.

"Listen, friend," began Maxi. "Pusspero is sick. You are our spare fighter. You must take his place."

The stranger did not answer.

I wasn't surprised. It was asking a lot.

"I'm talking to you!" hissed Maxi. "Pusspero is too sick to fight. He'll get killed out there."

"Spartan, help me!" yelled Maxi, as he sprang across the bench and grabbed the stranger by the helmet. The stranger made no attempt to resist. Slowly, the helmet came off.

"Furia!" I gasped. "I thought you'd escaped."

"I did," she hissed.

"What happened?" I gasped.

"They caught me," she answered. "Perhaps the Father has spies. Or perhaps one of my so called 'friends' from school betrayed me?"

There was no time to take offence.

"Listen Furia," I said. "They want to watch new fighters. Pusspero is too sick. Will you fight?"

"No," she said quietly. "Don't ask."

"It's Pusspero's life we are talking about. The giant will destroy him."

"I'm sorry," said Furia. "I can't help."

"Coward!" hissed Maxi. "You Hisspanians are all the same."

"You talk about courage," said Furia, glaring across the bench at Maxi. "But you know nothing. Nothing about courage. Nothing about Hisspania. Nothing about me."

"Please Furia," I begged. "Just listen to what I have to say."

I spoke in a whisper and Furia listened carefully to me.

A few minutes later Wulfren returned.

"Come on Pusspero," he growled. "The Father still says it has to be you."

"Wait!" I said. "Wait Wulfren. Please! Let me speak with the Father..."

"What are you waiting for?" growled a furious voice. It was the Father himself.

"Pusspero is ill," said Maxi.

"What of it?" asked the Father. "Sick or not, he must fight."

"Let one of us take his place," pleaded Maxi.

"Sorry," said the Father. "None of you will do. They've paid to watch different fighters."

Just then, Furia came forward.

"How about me?" she asked. "Will I do?"

Her orange eyes burned brighter than the Senator's torches.

"I am ready," she said softly.

The Father scratched his ear. He was wondering why she had suddenly changed her mind.

I sprang up and whispered into the Father's ear, explaining my plan.

"Are you ready to fight?" asked the Father.

Furia grabbed the trident and stalked off towards the edge of the arena.

"I think we can take that as a 'yes'," said Maxi.

"So be it!" said the Father.

He padded off. For a few minutes we waited nervously. Suddenly, he appeared again and introduced the fighters.

"Ambassador! Senator! Friends! Fighting for the honour of Cattage, I present the Beast from East Africa. The

Awesome Gigantipuss..."

I raced up to Furia.

"I wanted to give you this," I said quietly. Putting my paw into my pocket, I produced a small golden charm. "Look! It matches yours. Perhaps it will bring you luck."

"Stars of Asteria!" hissed Furia. She snatched the charm and grabbed me by the throat. "Where did you get THAT?"

"At the school..." I spluttered.

"That's enough!" ordered Wulfren, pulling Furia off me. "Save it for HIM!"

The giant from Cattage was lumbering around the arena. Father Felinious had to shout to make himself heard over the cheers from the crowd. They suddenly seemed to have woken up.

"And defending the honour of Rome tonight..."

Furia hissed when she heard this.

"... I give you... Furia of Hisspania."

The crowd gasped. How could a tiny female take on this brute from Cattage? The guests chattered in excitement. Large amounts of money changed paws. The drums began to beat and the trumpeter blew a lonely blast on his instrument. Meanwhile, Furia waited silently in the centre of the ring.

"Paws save her!" said Maxi, turning to me. "Spartan – what have we done?"

The giant lumbered forwards, raised his sword and swung it. There was a whizzing noise as the broad blade ripped through the air. Furia didn't move her feet. She dipped slightly, like a reed on a riverbank, caught by a gust of wind. The sword flashed past Furia's face, missing her ear by a whisker. The giant laughed.

"Run!" he boomed. "Run little one while you still have legs."

Furia glared back at him. He moved closer, raised his gladius again and took another swipe. The sword arced towards Furia. This time she moved a whisker to the left. The crowd gasped again.

"What's happening?" called Pusspero.

"He can't hit her!" cried Maxi excitedly. "Furia is winning the fight!"

"Thank Mewpiter! coughed Pusspero.

But the giant came at Furia again. This time he tried to smash her with his paw. Furia only needed a single step this time. The blow passed harmlessly to her right.

The giant tried again, this time he aimed a sweeping blow at her legs. Furia dodged it with a graceful leap.

"Stand still female!" growled the giant, swiping at her once again.

He was puffing and blowing. His fights didn't usually last this long.

"We females prefer dancing to standing still," laughed Furia. "Do you want to dance with me?"

Furia put down her trident and began to clap out a catchy rhythm.

Clap clap! Clap clap! Clap clap!

The crowd heard this and they began to join in. Soon the rhythm echoed around the courtyard.

Furia turned to the musicians.

"Hey Romans! Do you know any tunes from Hisspania? Or did you leave our music when you stole our gold?"

The musicians laughed and they struck up a bouncing tune that went well with the clapping.

"My thanks," she laughed. "Come on!"

Now the whole crowd had got the rhythm.

Clap clap! Clap clap! Clap clap!

The giant from Cattage looked puzzled. He ran his claws down his sword edge.

"She can't win by dodging," said Maxi. "She has to land some blows."

"Ready to dance?" laughed Furia, grabbing the trident and beckoning to him to step forward, as the crowd clapped loudly.

The giant looked worried. His tail was as thick as a drain pipe, but it began to thump nervously against the sand.

"Are you afraid to dance with Furia?" she said, shaking her head. "Or is this what you're frightened of?"

She waved the trident towards him.

"Actually, I don't even need a spear for this."

Furia drew back her arm and threw her trident. It sailed through the air and slammed into the wooden fence. Then she padded over towards one of the slaves and grabbed a broom.

"Ready to dance now?" she asked.

This drew howls of laughter from the crowd. The Father sat stone faced like a temple statue. Every eye in the place waited for the dance to begin.

Clap clap clap! Clap clap clap!

This time it was Furia who advanced. She walked forward and thrust the broom towards the face of her enemy.

The giant stuck out a paw the size of a dinner plate. He tried to grab the broom but Furia flicked it into his face, sending him scrabbling to protect his eyes. Then she sprang at his legs and heaved. He hung in the air for a moment, flapping like a flag on a pole, before toppling into the sand with a mighty thud and a grunt.

Furia snatched the gladius from his shaking paw. She leapt up onto the giant's chest. Victory was hers.

The crowd roared and clapped and whistled.

"Hisspania! Furia!" they chanted.

But there was no celebration from their winner. The smile had vanished from Furia's face She stalked silently back and took her seat beside us.

"You were... amazing!" I said.

"Thank you Furia," said Pusspero. "One day I will repay the favour."

"Remember his words," said Maxi. The Sons of Paws never forget a good turn."

MAUIS XX

May 20th

The thrill of yesterday's fight has blown away like smoke on the breeze. Today I licked my wounds. Every muscle in my body ached. Maxi didn't seem to be feeling it.

"Spartan," he began, as we made our way towards the canteen.

"What?" I replied.

"There's one thing I don't understand. How did you talk Furia into fighting last night?"

"Stop calling me 'Spartan' and I might tell you," I replied.

"It's a deal," laughed Maxi. "You have my word on it."

"Well," I explained, "I knew that the Senator wanted us to LOSE."

"How did you know that?" he asked.

"I heard him talking to his slaves. Didn't you think it was odd that the whole crowd were cheering for Cattage?"

"Yes, that was strange," said Maxi.

"They were ordered to support Cattage," I explained.

"But that still doesn't explain how you got Furia to agree to fight."

I didn't understand cats like Maxi. At first, I'd taken him for a bully. He was a born show off and he loved the sound of his own voice. He had spent most of the last week annoying me and teasing Pusspero. But when it really mattered, he had volunteered to fight in Pusspero's place. I decided that I could trust him.

"All right," I said. "I'll try to explain. But Furia must never find out."

"I'll be as silent as Hissy-khia," he whispered.

My tail began to flick.

"Who?" I moaned.

"She's the Squeak Spirit of Silence," he explained. "I promise I won't say a word. Go on!"

"I told Furia the truth," I said.

"What do you mean?" asked Maxi.

"Furia hates Rome and everything it stands for."

Maxi let out a surprised hiss.

"I told Furia that the Senator WANTED our team to lose. So if she won the fight, it would be a victory AGAINST Rome."

A hollow bell rang out. The day's training was about to begin. Soon we would hear the familiar sound of swords clashing against spears.

There was still no sign of Furia. I wondered if she was going to try to escape again. I didn't understand her. Why had she become so angry when I gave her the golden charm? These thoughts were interrupted by another question from Maxi.

"What about Father Felinious?" he asked. "What did you say to him? How did you persuade him to let Furia fight?"

I smiled, feeling pleased with myself.

"Felinious was desperate to watch Furia fight," I explained. "And I told him that if he bet on Furia defeating the giant, he could win himself a fortune."

"That's clever thinking..." laughed Maxi, "...for a Spartan."

The Olympuss Games

Follow the adventures of Son of Spartapuss and his fiery companion Furia from gladiator school to the foot of Mount Olympuss.

Son of Spartapuss

BOOK I   ISBN: 9781906132811

New to Rome, the son of Spartapuss (nicknamed S.O.S.) has a lot to learn. When a mysterious stranger pays his debts, he finds himself in a school for gladiators.

Eye of the Cyclaw

BOOK II   ISBN: 9781906132835

The Son of Spartapuss discovers that his friend Furia is on a secret quest. Meanwhile, the trials for the Olympuss Games begin. To win a place, S.O.S. must defeat the fearsome gladiator known as The Cyclaw.

Maze of the Minopaw

BOOK III   ISBN: 9781906132842

On route to the Olympuss Games, the Son of Spartapuss and Furia get mixed up in an ancient mystery. Can they escape from a monstrous danger?

Stars of Olympuss

BOOK IV   ISBN: 9781906132828

As Furia's quest reaches an end, the Squeaks are holding the biggest games ever. But the Roman Emperor Nero has made some terrifying changes to make the games more exciting.

WWW.MOGZILLA.CO.UK/SHOP

The original Spartapuss series is set in ancient Rome, in a world ruled by cats.

I Am Spartapuss
BOOK I

Spartapuss, a ginger cat, is happy managing Rome's most famous Bath & Spa. But Fortune has other plans for him.
ISBN: 9780954657604

Catligula
BOOK II

When Catligula becomes Emperor, his madness brings Rome to within a whisker of disaster.
ISBN: 9780954657611

Die Clawdius
BOOK III

The Emperor Clawdius decides to invade Spartapuss' home – The Land of the Kitons.

ISBN: 9780954657680

Boudicat
BOOK IV

Queen Boudicat has declared war on Rome and she wants Spartapuss to join her rebel army.
ISBN: 9781906132019

Cleocatra's Kushion
BOOK V

Spartapuss must travel through Fleagypt to the land of the Kushites and find his missing son.
ISBN: 9781906132064

WWW.MOGZILLA.CO.UK/SHOP